Alexandra the Royal Baby Fairy was originally published
as a Rainbow Magic special. This version has
been specially adapted for developing readers
in conjunction with a Reading Consultant.

Extra-special thanks
to Sarah Levison

Reading Consultant: Prue Goodwin, lecturer in literacy and children's books.

ORCHARD BOOKS
Carmelite House, 50 Victoria Embankment, London EC4Y 0DZ.
*Orchard Books Australia*
Level 17/207 Kent Street, Sydney, NSW 2000

This text first published in 2013 by Orchard Books
This Early Reader edition published in 2016
© 2016 Rainbow Magic Limited.
© 2016 HIT Entertainment Limited.

Illustrations © Orchard Books 2016

HiT entertainment

A CIP catalogue record for this book is available from the British Library.

ISBN 978 1 40834 029 5

1 3 5 7 9 10 8 6 4 2

Printed in China

MIX
Paper from
responsible sources
FSC
www.fsc.org   FSC® C104740

The paper and board used in this book are made from wood from responsible sources

Orchard Books is an imprint of Hachette Children's Group and published by
the Watts Publishing Group Limited, an Hachette UK company.

www.hachette.co.uk

# Alexandra
## the Royal Baby
## Fairy

by Daisy Meadows

ORCHARD

www.rainbowmagic.co.uk

The Fairyland Palace

Seeing Pool

Royal Nursery

NORWOOD PALACE

Jack Frost's Ice Castle

Throne Room

Wetherbury Village

# Contents

Story One:    The Adventure Begins         9

Story Two:    The Rescue Mission          31

Story Three:  The Happy Family            55

# Story One

## The Adventure Begins

# Chapter One

# The Royal Palace

"Mum, are we nearly there?" asked Kirsty. She felt like they had been in the car for ages!

Mrs Tate smiled at Kirsty and her best friend Rachel Walker. "We're almost at Norwood Palace, girls! Look, there it is."

The girls gasped as they saw

a beautiful building ahead of them. It was made from golden stone and surrounded by smart gardens.

"Wow!" cried Rachel as the car pulled into the drive.

Rachel was staying with her best friend Kirsty for the spring half-term holidays. Mrs Tate was a volunteer at Norwood Palace and today the girls were going to help with a children's open day.

Kirsty and Rachel had a very special secret: they were great

friends with the fairies! They'd had lots of amazing adventures. They hoped they'd meet a new magical friend very soon!

Mrs Tate parked the car and opened the door for Rachel

and Kirsty. "OK, girls," she smiled, "I'll be in the royal kitchens today and you'll be in the royal nursery at the top of the house. I'm sure the visiting children will enjoy seeing where the royal babies

and children used to sleep and play!"

Mrs Tate gave the girls a map of the palace and some quizzes and colouring pages for the visitors. "I'll come up and see you soon," she said.

"Thanks, Mum!" cried Kirsty, grabbing Rachel's hand. They couldn't wait to explore the palace!

The girls ran up the grand staircase to the first floor of the palace. There were lots of beautiful paintings and

tapestries on the walls. They
raced along the wide corridors
and soon they reached a smaller
set of stairs leading right up to
the top of the palace.

"Can you imagine growing
up here?" smiled Rachel as

they climbed the stairs. "There are so many places to play. Oh, Kirsty, look!"

# Chapter Two

## Alexandra Appears!

The girls had reached the royal nursery. The room had a sloped ceiling, which made it feel very cosy. The room was decorated in soft pink and blue stripes. Pretty pictures of animals hung on the walls and there were lots of toys everywhere!

"Look at this doll!" cried Rachel, carefully picking up a china doll. "She looks like Kate the Royal Wedding Fairy!"

Kirsty opened a book called Fairy Stories from Around the World. "What a lovely book. Although I'm sure our adventures with the fairies are even more exciting than the ones in here!"

As Kirsty closed the book, a cloud of dust flew up into the air. Then the dust whirled around Rachel and Kirsty.

The girls could see nothing but a cloud of sparkles! When it finally settled, it revealed a tiny fairy. She did a loop-the-loop in the air and flew towards them.

"Hello, girls!" the fairy cried. "I'm Alexandra the Royal Baby Fairy!"

Alexandra was wearing a beautiful pink dress with a silk bow at the waist. She had wavy auburn hair that came down over her shoulder in a loose plait, and a pretty pendant hanging around her neck.

"Hello, Alexandra!" chorused the girls. How exciting to meet a new fairy friend!

"Do you look after all royal babies, Alexandra?" asked Rachel.

"Yes," smiled Alexandra, landing on Kirsty's shoulder.

"Whenever a new royal baby arrives I am there to greet them," she explained. "I give each of them my magical silver rattle to hold. This makes sure that the royal baby has a wonderful childhood.

Then they will enjoy all their royal duties as they get older!"

But then Alexandra's smile faded, and she buried her little face in her hands.

"Girls," she said sadly. "Something awful has happened!"

"Oh, no!" cried Rachel, "has something happened to your magic rattle?"

Alexandra shook her head sadly. "My magic rattle is safe. It's the new royal baby that's missing!"

# Chapter Three

## A trip to Fairyland

Kirsty and Rachel couldn't believe what they were hearing!

"How did the royal baby go missing?" cried Kirsty.

"Well, Princess Grace and Prince Arthur were waiting for their baby to be delivered by Foster, the head stork," Alexandra explained. "Foster delivers all Fairyland babies to their parents. But he's gone missing and nobody knows where he is!"

"Shall we help you to find out what's going on?" Rachel asked.

"Yes, please!" cried Alexandra. "Will you come to Fairyland with me? Time will stand still here whilst you're away."

"Of course we will!" chorused the girls. They could hardly wait to start a new adventure!

Alexandra waved her wand and a glittering whirlwind

surrounded the three friends. Rachel and Kirsty felt themselves growing smaller, with floaty wings upon their backs.

A moment later they landed outside the Fairyland Palace. A group of fairies were there, including King Oberon and Queen Titania, rulers of Fairyland.

"Rachel and Kirsty, thank you for coming to help us," said King Oberon. "We have created a seeing pool to try to find out what happened to Foster and the royal baby."

The seeing pool showed
a white stork landing by a
gooseberry bush. Underneath the
bush was the adorable royal baby,
wrapped snugly in a blanket.
Foster carefully picked up the
baby bundle and flew away.

Next, the seeing pool showed a strange creature on the ground. It had scruffy wings, a big beak and was covered in a large sheet. It was screeching loudly! Kind Foster landed beside the strange creature to see if it needed any help.

Suddenly, Jack Frost appeared from underneath the sheet. The creature was Jack Frost in disguise! The Ice Lord grabbed Foster and the baby and muttered a spell. In a bright-blue flash, they disappeared.

The seeing pool clouded over.

"I can't believe it!" cried Alexandra. "Why would Jack Frost take Foster and the royal baby?"

Kirsty and Rachel looked at each other. "There's only one thing for it," said Kirsty. "We need to visit the Ice Castle and find out what Jack Frost is up to!"

# Story Two

# The Rescue Mission

# Chapter Four

## Into the Ice Castle!

Rachel, Kirsty and Alexandra flew off towards the spooky Ice Castle. After a few minutes, the three friends saw the tall turrets of Jack Frost's home.

Icy cold mist curled around their wings as they spotted an open window on the side of the castle. The three fairies flew up and went through the window into the castle. Luckily the goblin guards didn't spot them as they were too busy squabbling!

"Alexandra, will you know when the royal baby is nearby?" asked Kirsty, as they flew along a corridor.

"I think so," said Alexandra. "And if the baby is crying, we'll all be able to hear it!"

Suddenly, they heard squawking coming from behind huge double doors. Squeezing their way into the room they saw a spiky throne. Hanging above the throne was a small cage, and in the cage was a large white bird with big, sad eyes.

"Oh, Foster, you poor thing!" cried Alexandra, flying straight up to the cage. "These are my friends, Kirsty and Rachel. We've come to rescue you both! But where is the royal baby?"

"Oh, Alexandra," sniffed Foster. "I'm so glad to see you!"

"Can you tell us what happened, Foster?" said Rachel.

"Jack Frost didn't realize that I was carrying a baby," whimpered Foster. "He was spying on some fairies and he heard them saying how

precious my delivery would
be. He thought I was carrying
fairy treasure!"

"Do you know where Jack
Frost took the baby?" asked
Kirsty urgently.

"No," replied the stork. "He shut me in this cage as soon as we got here."

Alexandra waved her wand and the cage door opened. "Foster, you must fly back to the palace and let the king and queen know you are all right."

"OK, but I'll come back soon!" cried Foster, flying shakily out of the window. The three fairy friends set off to search the rest of the castle.

After a few minutes they heard a strange noise coming

from one of the rooms. Flying
over to the door, the three
friends peered through.

In front of them was a very
strange sight! There were lots
of goblins in the room. One
was juggling, one was eating

bogmallows and another
was drawing pictures on a
blackboard. And in the middle
of the room was the beautiful
royal baby!

# Chapter Five

# Goblin
# Teacher

Alexandra, Kirsty and Rachel flew into the room and hid behind an armchair.

The plump goblin eating the bogmallows gave a huge burp. "Silly baby!" he moaned. "It won't wake up and learn how to eat bogmallows!"

"I know," agreed the goblin by the blackboard. "I'm trying to teach it all my best tricks!"

"Stop whinging!" screeched a tall goblin. "The boss said we have to try and teach it how to be sneaky. Then when it grows up, it'll be able to play mean tricks on the fairies!"

Safely hidden behind the armchair, the fairies gasped.

Jack Frost had decided to make
the baby part of his sneaky
goblin gang!

Just then, the baby started crying.

"Do something!" cried a
small goblin, putting his hands
over his ears. "Make it stop!"

The goblins seemed scared

to go near the baby.
One of the goblins
tried juggling balls
of mud close to
the baby's head,
but that made it
cry even more!

"Oh, I can't stand it!" cried Alexandra. And before Kirsty or Rachel could stop her, the brave little fairy flew right up to the goblins!

"This little baby needs to be with its mummy and daddy," shouted brave Alexandra, "not with you goblins – you are upsetting it!"

The goblins looked ashamed.

"We didn't mean to," one of
them whined, hanging his
head. "It doesn't act like a
goblin baby!"

"Well of course it doesn't,"
scolded Alexandra. "That's
because this is a royal fairy
baby!" She smiled down at the

baby, who gazed at Alexandra with big, beautiful eyes. "How would you feel if a little goblin baby was kept away from its mummy and daddy?"

Rachel and Kirsty heard a strange gurgling sound. They realised that some of the goblins were crying!

"We were being nice to
it!" sobbed the plump goblin.
"I tried to give it one of my
bogmallows!"

Alexandra looked at the

goblins kindly. "I know you were trying your best. But this baby needs to be with fairies, not goblins! I'm going to take this baby to its mummy and daddy." And Alexandra flew towards the baby.

"Aha! I don't think so," came an icy voice from the doorway. It was Jack Frost!

# Chapter Six

## Jack Frost's Soft Side!

The mean Ice Lord pointed his
wand at Alexandra and a bolt of
icy magic zoomed out, freezing
the poor fairy in midair!

Jack Frost stalked into the
centre of the room. "I might have
known you silly fairies would
appear," he hissed. "Well, I'm

going to teach you all a lesson!"
Jack Frost pointed his wand at
Kirsty and Rachel and they felt
their wings begin to freeze.

Suddenly, the royal fairy
baby stretched its tiny wings
and flew into Jack Frost's arms.
The mean Ice Lord started to

act very strangely… he seemed to like the royal baby!

"Who is a cute little fairy wairy?" Jack Frost cooed. "Yes you are! Hey diddly doo, Uncle Jack loves you!"

As the Ice Lord bent over to tickle the baby, the tiny fairy grabbed the wand. Magic bolts started to shoot from it, zooming around the room!

One bolt hit a goblin and he shrank to the size of a mouse. Another trapped two goblins in the middle of a large snowball!

One of the magical sparks hit
Alexandra, breaking the spell.
She flew towards the girls.

"Look, Alexandra," said
Kirsty, "Jack Frost is being very
nice to the baby!"

Jack Frost had managed

to get his wand back from
the royal baby and was now
singing a silly nursery rhyme.

"But how are we going to
get the baby away from Jack
Frost?" said Alexandra.

"I think I know what we can

do," said Rachel. "Let's try to make Jack Frost see how hard it will be to look after a little baby. And tell him it will be a very long time before the baby can learn any mean tricks!"

"That's a great plan!" said Kirsty. "And I think I know what else we can say to persuade him. Let's hope it works and then we can return the royal baby to its mummy and daddy!"

# Story Three

## The Happy Family

# Chapter Seven

# A Perfect Plan

The Ice Lord scowled at the
fairies as they flew over to
him. "Go away!" he snapped,
cuddling the royal baby. "Can't
you see I'm busy?"

"Oh, this isn't busy!" said
Alexandra brightly. "The
baby will need to be fed soon,

and then its nappy will need changing. Then it will need a sleep, then another feed and another nappy change! And it will wake up lots in the night too, so you won't get much sleep."

Jack Frost turned a paler shade of blue. "But I need my beauty sleep," he muttered. "I don't like to be disturbed by anyone! And I get very grumpy if I don't have a lie-in every day." He looked at the little baby with a frown.

"You're so good with the

baby," said Rachel kindly. "It obviously likes you very much! But this little one needs lots of looking after and special care. What if you had another baby to play with, one that's easier to look after?"

"Hmmn, well that does sound like quite a good idea," said Jack Frost. He looked around him at the mess that the baby had made, then glared at the fairies. "But where is the other baby? How do I know you're not playing tricks on me?"

Alexandra waved her wand in the air and smiled at the Ice Lord. "The new baby is outside, let's go and meet it!"

The three fairies and Jack Frost headed outside to the frozen pond. Jack Frost was holding on to the royal baby tightly.

"You lied!" screeched the icy creature, looking all around him. "There are no other babies here for me to play with. I'm keeping this one!"

"Wait! Look over there!" cried Alexandra, pointing at

the horizon. The girls and Jack Frost looked at the sky and saw a shape coming towards them, but what was it…?

# Chapter Eight

## A Royal Delivery

As the three fairies and Jack
Frost peered into the sky, they
soon saw that a beautiful
white bird was flying towards
them. It was Foster, carrying a
new baby bundle in his beak!
the stork landed carefully on
the icy ground by Jack Frost's

flock of snow geese and one
snow goose immediately came
forward. It was Jack Frost's
precious pet! Foster put his
baby bundle down on the
ground. A moment later, out of
the bundle waddled a beautiful,
snow goose chick.

The cute baby bird was covered in soft grey fluff and cheeped loudly as it stretched its tiny wings.

"Oh! My precious snow goose has had a baby!" cried the Ice Lord, jumping up and down with joy. He quickly handed over the royal baby to Alexandra and ran over to greet the snow goose chick. The snow geese family were very pleased to see him!

"Hello, sweetie!" whispered Alexandra to the royal baby,

who was looking up at her
happily. "It's so nice to meet
you properly at last!"

Alexandra waved her wand
in the air. The air shimmered
for a moment and then

Alexandra's beautiful silver
rattle appeared. She put the
rattle in the royal baby's tiny
hand and the little fairy shook
it up and down.

A beautiful tinkling noise came from the rattle and a mist of magical sparkles surrounded the baby. The little royal baby gurgled happily, smiled at Alexandra and the girls and then settled down to sleep.

"Hurrah!" cried Rachel and Kirsty, giving each other and Alexandra a huge hug. They had the royal baby back at last!

"Let's leave this freezing place and take the baby back to the Fairyland Palace!" said Alexandra happily. Rachel and

Kirsty squeezed each other's hands. "Who'd have thought that Jack Frost could be such a softy?" laughed Rachel. "I know!" agreed Kirsty. "It seems that babies really do bring out the best in everyone. Even an Ice Lord!"

# Chapter Nine

## Home
## At Last!

Foster picked up the sleeping
baby in his beak and the friends
flew towards the sparkling pink
turrets of the Fairyland Palace.
It was so nice to feel the warm
sunshine on their wings!

When they reached the
palace, the friends saw a large

group gathered to greet them. There was King Oberon and Queen Titania, and Prince Arthur and Princess Grace were jumping up and down with excitement! A group of fairy children were waving a sparkly banner that read 'Welcome Home Your Highness!'

As the fairies and Foster landed, the crowd parted to let Princess Grace and Prince Arthur come to the front. The royal couple had tears in their eyes as Alexandra gave a deep

curtsey and handed over the
royal baby to them. The little
fairy baby opened its eyes and
cooed happily at its mummy
and daddy. The watching

fairies started cheering and with a wave of his royal wand, King Oberon created magic fireworks that whizzed around the dusky sky, bursting with every colour of the rainbow!

"Dearest Rachel and Kirsty, thank you so much for helping us again!" smiled Queen Titania.

"It was our pleasure!" said
Kirsty with a huge smile.

"We just love helping our
fairy friends," added Rachel.

Soon it was time for the girls
to return to Norwood Palace.
They held hands as they whizzed
back to the royal nursery. Time
had stood still in the human
world, and some children soon
arrived to explore the palace.

"Phew, what an exciting day!"
said Rachel as the two girls left
the palace later that afternoon.
"Oh, look, there's your mum."

Mrs Tate was on her mobile phone, looking very happy. She finished her call and turned to the girls. "Hi, girls! I've just had some exciting news. Kirsty, your cousin Esther has had her baby! We're going to visit them on the way home. What a treat to see such a tiny baby!"

The two girls smiled at each other. "Rachel, can you believe we're going to meet two new babies in one day?" whispered Kirsty.

"I know," smiled Rachel,

squeezing her best friend's hand. "And one of them was a royal fairy baby! This really has been one of the most magical adventures ever. I can't wait for the next one!"

The End

**If you enjoyed this story, you may want to read**

# Kate the Royal Wedding Fairy Early Reader

**Here's how the story begins...**

"Spring is my favourite season," said Rachel Walker, swinging her roller-skates happily.

"And mine," said her best friend Kirsty Tate. "I love seeing all the bright flowers."

Kirsty was spending half term in Tippington with Rachel and

they had been roller-skating in
the park all morning.

"I wonder what's for lunch,"
said Kirsty. "All that skating
has made me really hungry."

"Me too," said Rachel.
Suddenly she stopped and
stared at one of the flowerbeds
in surprise.

"What's the matter?" asked
Kirsty, stopping as well.

"Look at that rose," said
Rachel. "There's something odd
about it . . ."

All the other flowers were

nodding and bowing in the
light spring breeze, but one
deep red rose wasn't moving.
It was standing up very tall and
stiff, like a soldier on parade.

Read
Kate the Royal Wedding Fairy
Early Reader
to find out what happens next!

# Meet the first seven
# Rainbow Magic fairies

Ruby
the Red
Fairy

Amber
the Orange
Fairy

Saffron
the Yellow
Fairy

Fern
the Green
Fairy

Sky
the Blue
Fairy

Izzy
the Indigo
Fairy

Heather
the Violet
Fairy

**There's a fairy book for everyone at:**
## www.rainbowmagicbooks.co.uk

Become a
Rainbow Magic
fairy friend and be the first to
see sneak peeks of new books.

There are lots of special offers and exclusive
competitions to win sparkly
Rainbow Magic prizes.

Sign up today at
**www.rainbowmagicbooks.co.uk**